Best Selling Authors
Steve Miller & Lizzy Stevens
With
Jason & Noah Miller

Don't Make A Wish

Solstice Publishing -
www.solsticepublishing.com

Don't Make A Wish

By

Lizzy Stevens & Steve Miller

With

Jason & Noah Miller

Chapter One

*T*ara West got up ready to start her day. It was strange walking through the house and not hearing her grandma making noise in the kitchen. No sounds of an off tune song being sung could be heard from down the hall. The house was quiet. Even though things were different she wanted to get started. It was going to be a busy day. First she had to call her boss and let him know that she wouldn't be into work for a couple of weeks off. It would take some time to get the funeral taken care of and things in order. She wanted to get started making lists of everything she planned to keep. She, of course, wanted to keep special things that held the dearest memories, but the rest she would try and sell in one big yard sale. What she could sell would help her with money and the rest would be donated. Her grandma had left her house to her and all her belongings since there was no other family to speak of.

There was way too much in the house for one person. Her grandma had collected things for years. Tara had made jokes of her being a pack rat over her lifetime.

The attic was going to be a huge undertaking. As she walked up the dim lit staircase; memories of playing up there as a child ran wild in her mind. There were book shelves on every wall and boxes filled the floor. Tara let out a loud sigh. "This is going to be a job." She said. She sat her pen and paper down on one of the boxes and walked around the room rummaging others. Basically looking to see what all was in them because nothing was marked on the outside of them.

Tara picked up several small boxes and was going to stack them up in the corner to get them out of the way. Walking over to sit them down she tripped over something on the floor and stumbled. Boxes flew out of her hands and she grabbed at the shelf on the wall. It went tumbling down making a crashing noise. "Oh Man! What a mess!" As she was getting up something caught her attention behind the shelf. She reached back and grabbed it. In her hand was an old antique style lamp. She wasn't sure what kind it was exactly but thought it might be worth something. Maybe it was an oil lamp of some kind. It wasn't anything she had ever seen before. Attached to the handle of it was a handwritten note from her grandmother.

"Whoever finds this lamp, Take my advice. Do not rub the lamp. Do not make a wish. Put it back where you found it and run away."

Tara turned the paper front and backwards and looked around the room as if there was somebody watching her as if this was some kind of joke. "What in the world Grandma?" She laughed. "Ok this might be worth something. I'll have to take this to get appraised. This will help the children's hospital in town a lot if it's worth something." She said.

Tara grabbed an old shirt out of one of the boxes and quickly wiped some of the dust off of the lamp so she could see what exactly it looked like.

Suddenly, smoke started coming from the spout of the lamp and it started to tremble in her hand. She set it down on the floor in front of her and stepped back.

Moments later in front of her stood a tall, tanned, dark haired, guy somewhat muscular wearing a red tank top, jeans and tennis shoes. "I'm Mark. I'm the Genie of the lamp. What are your 3 wishes?"

Tara stood there in a shocked state for a minute. "Wait. What?" Was all she could get out.

"Okay, I see. I need to go slow with you." He said. "I am Mark. You have my lamp." He pointed to the lamp. "You" He pointed to Tara. "Rubbed the lamp. I" He pointed to himself. "Am here. You now tell me your 3 wishes. I give them to you and then I get to go back into my lamp and I get to be left alone. See how this works? Real simple. Give me your greedy little wishes and let's be done with this."

Tara forgot the fact that there was somebody in her attic that just poofed out of a lamp and calling himself a genie. She was more than angry that he was in her house using his arrogant attitude with her and acting like he was superior to her. "Excuse me Mr. I am better than everyone with my leave me alone attitude. Why don't you just jump back into the lamp that you jumped out of? I have way too much on my plate to deal with the likes of you today."

Mark walked over to her with his hands on his hips. "I would love to do just that but I can't."

Tara kicked a box out of the way as she paced around the attic not really knowing what her plans were. "Why not?"

"Well, Genius. You rubbed my lamp. And as the rule has been around for centuries, when a genie's lamp has been activated the person who activated it is granted three wishes. I can't return to my lamp until I have granted those three wishes. So do us both a favor and just get your greed on and get this over with."

Tara had had about enough of his attitude. "I don't want your stupid wishes. So how about you give them to somebody else. I'm going to make me some dinner." She turned and went down the stairs.

"Wait." Mark said. "You can't do that. You can't not wish."

"Watch me." Tara said. As she stormed off to the kitchen to make her some dinner. It had been a rough couple of days and she was not in the mood to put up with some jerk.

Tara walked into the kitchen and over to the refrigerator. She saw so many casserole dishes in there from her grandma's funeral yesterday. *Why does everyone think food is so conforming to a person grieving? She thought to herself.* Everyone brought something for her grandma's service. She felt a little hint of guilt hit her. "Mark, do genies eat? I have plenty of food if you would like a plate."

"That's kind of stupid question. Of course we eat." He said.

Tara rolled her eyes. "Okay. Sit down and I'll fix you a plate real fast. Then I have to take a bunch of food over to the Pastor by eleven so he can get it to the homeless shelter in town by lunch time. What are you planning on doing? I mean where are you going? I'm not making wishes and you can't go back in your lamp and you can't just live with me forever. So what's the plan here?"

Mark let out a frustrated sigh. "What is your problem? Just make the wishes so we can be done with this."

Tara turned around and gave him an evil mean look. "What is my problem? What is my problem? Oh you don't even have time to hear my problems? But let's start with you. You pop out of a lamp that I was just dusting. I wasn't looking for a genie and I sure the heck wasn't looking for some jerk to pop out in a tank top and jeans. I mean seriously. What is that? And then you use some hateful attitude with me and try and force me to make wishes that I don't even want to begin with. I don't have time for this stupid stuff. I actually have a life. I don't have time for this make believe fairytale dream life stuff. It's not real. You can't just wish for stuff and poof there it is. So no I'm not interested."

Mark just stood there looking at her. "Okay then. So about those wishes. Can you just make one?"

Tara threw a fork in the sink as hard as she could and it crashed into a glass and broke it. "Fine. What I would like is for you to make all the kids at the children's hospital in town that I volunteer at better so they can all go home today. That's my wish. That's what I would like right now."

Mark looked at her with a confused look. "I'm sorry, but that's against the rules. It can't be done."

"What?" Tara asked. "I don't understand. You have been on me this whole time to make a wish. Make a wish. And when I do you tell me I can't have it. That's just great. Thanks a lot."

Mark stomped his foot. "Stop being difficult. You want your wish to be a wish for an entire hospital. Just make three simple wishes so I can leave this horrible place."

Tara turned around and started packaging up the food. "I don't have time for this." She started slamming food into cardboard boxes angrily. She was tiring fast of his attitude. "I have got to get the food over to the shelter so everyone can eat. You need to be gone when I get back." She turned and left her house with her arms full of food.

Chapter Two

Tara hadn't seen Mark in a couple of days and hoped that meant he was gone; but the noise downstairs let her know she was wrong.

"Honey. I'm home." Mark sang out from downstairs."

Tara sat up in her bed, ran her hand through her hair. "Ugh. He's back." She balled up her fist and hit the bed. The blankets hit the floor as she got out of bed and she stomped down the stairs.

"What are you doing here? I thought you left." She shot him an uninviting glare. "And why are you in my house?" She walked into the kitchen and right to the coffee pot.

"I told you I can't leave until I grant you three wishes." Mark said.

Tara stomped back over in front of him. "Oh, no, you don't. I tried to make a wish and you wouldn't do it. So what you mean is you will only grant me the wishes you want to grant. There is a big difference. Now isn't there?"

Mark shook his head. "Don't be stubborn. You can end this for both of us if you would just make the wishes. I don't want to be here anymore than you want me to be here. So just make the wishes and I'm gone. It's that easy."

Tara walked back to the kitchen and poured herself a cup of coffee. "Fine. If it will get you out of here. Give me the coolest truck in town. That will actually help me out a lot. So if you are going to give me a new truck it might as well be a cool one." Tara said smiling.

Mark jumped up. "Finally. Yes! It's outside in the driveway waiting for you."

Tara looked up at him in shock. "Are you serious? That fast?"

Mark nodded. "Yep. That's how it works. I am a Genie."

Tara jumped up and gave him a little hug. "This is actually going to help me a lot. I didn't want to take it but, I do deliveries in the day for the nursing home in town. A lot of the patients there don't have any family and they all need big items picked up that will never fit in my car so I need a truck. On top of that my car is just about on its last leg. I was hoping to get enough money from the yard sale to get a used car from the lot in town. I don't need anything fancy. Just something to get me back and forth and pick up and deliver their stuff. So this will be perfect." Tara went running out the door.

"Wait," Mark yelled.

Tara stopped mid run. Sitting in the middle of her drive way was one of those box trucks for delivering ice to grocery stores. She turned to face Mark and bent down and picked up a rock from the driveway. She threw the rock at him. "Really? You think you are funny don't you. The coolest truck in town. Really? You got me an ice delivery truck. Really?" Tara bent down and grabbed more rocks and started throwing them at him.

Mark was dodging them right and left. "Wait. I'm sorry, but it is a little funny. It is the coolest truck. Right? Come on. It is a little funny."

Tara walked past him pushing him aside on her way in. She walked into the house and grabbed her purse.

"Where are you going? Mark asked.

She gave him one of those drop dead looks. "I really don't see how what I do is any of your business. Why don't you go away?"

Mark smiled. "I can't. You have two more wishes."

Tara let out a sigh and pushed her hair out of her face. "I don't want my wishes. Give them to somebody else."

"Can't. It's against the rules." He said.

"Then I wish you would go away." She said."

"Can't do that. It doesn't count. It has to be an actual wish. You can't wish me away."

"Ugh. I hate you." Tara turned to leave.

Mark stepped in front of her. "Wait. I'm sorry. Really where are you going. You're upset. I don't want you to leave upset."

"I'm fine. I'm just taking your lovely little gift down to Mr. Johnson at that small convenience store on the corner. His truck broke down last year and he hasn't had the money to get a new one. Obviously I don't need an ice truck so I'm going to go give it to him." She looked over at the confused look on Mark's face.

Mark started pacing back and forth. "What is up with you? You are not going to throw a fit? Scream? Yell? Cry? Anything? You are just going to go give it away? Okay well that was fun."

A sad look came across Tara's face. "I've done enough crying this week." She picked up the keys to the truck. "Don't wait up. Go do whatever it is you do. I don't have time to mess with anymore wishes today. I will be at the church until late tonight. My grandma volunteered there every night for the ladies and I don't want to let them down tonight. So I said I would fill in. I'm going to host it for them tonight."

"Well why can't your grandma do it if she's the one that volunteers for it? What is with people?"

Tara's eyes filled will tears instantly. "Are you serious right now? Would you please just go? Just give the stupid wishes to somebody else. I don't want them. Give me something to sign saying I don't want them. I never wanted them." She turned and walked out the door."

* * *

Tara was busy over the past few days and hadn't spent much time thinking about Mark or the wishes. He wasn't anywhere to be seen so maybe he was finally out of her life for good was what she was thinking. That thought suddenly changed when she walked into the living room and saw him standing there.

She walked in and stopped mid walk. "What are you doing here? I told you to give the last two wishes away."

Mark put his hands on his hips. "And I told you it doesn't work that way. Now you have wasted enough of my time. It's time to get this over with. Make your damn wishes so I can move on with my life. I have had enough of your games."

Tara was wearing a pair of running pants and a yellow tank top. She walked into the kitchen to fill up a sports bottle with ice and water. "Fine. I wish I had a pair of shoes that'll make me look like I'm on fire."

Mark smiled really big and rubbed his hands together. He snapped his finger and said "There."

Tara looked down and yelled. "Oh my God. What have you done?" She was wearing a pair of tennis shoes that were literally on fire. Flames were coming from her shoes. She kicked them off, grabbed a blanket, wrapped them up in it and ran them to the kitchen sink and put the fire out.

"I don't know what is wrong with you but you have ruined everything. Now I'm late."

Mark shook his head. "What, late for a run in the park? You are stick thin, but I

17

guess you have to work on your figure some more. So shallow."

"You don't know me. I was running in the marathon today to raise money for charity. Thanks for ruining it for me though. That was great. I'm sure the kids will get the money from other runners."

Mark hesitated then stammered a bit. "Look I'm giving you what you ask for. You should be clearer. You have one more wish. Just get it over with and I'll be out of your life."

Words couldn't describe how angry Tara was at that moment. "Okay I can't be any more clear about this wish. My third and final wish is this. I wish you would leave me alone. There you go. There it is."

Mark jumped up. "And you shall have it."

Smoke started to appear. Tara felt herself spinning. She was going in circles. She didn't know what was happening. She felt herself drop to the ground. Sand was under her feet. She looked around. She could see water for miles. Palm trees with coconuts. Blue water was in front of her. Behind her she didn't know what she would find. *I hope this is a friendly island.* She said to nobody.

18

The more she looked around the madder she got. "Mark you no good son of ugh. Really? Leave me alone? Really? You think this is funny? How do I get out of here? How do I get home from here?"

Minutes later Tara heard a noise a few feet away and she looked around for some kind of weapon. She found a stick on the ground. It wasn't much but she grabbed it anyway. Not sure what she would do with a dry rotted stick but it made her feel better to hold onto it anyway.

Then she saw Mark come walking from behind the tree. "What are you doing? Did you think this was funny?"

Mark dusted off the sand from his jeans. "Well I actually did think it was kind of funny until I got in trouble and got sent here with you."

Tara tossed the stick down. "In trouble? What are you talking about? Zap us out of here."

Mark put his hands together and cracked his knuckles. "I can't."

"What do you mean you can't" Tara huffed.

"Well you see." Mark slowly started. "I can't. I have no powers. My bosses were not real happy with the granting of my wishes to you. Apparently it's not funny to light peoples' shoes on fire."

Tara couldn't help but smile. "Really? Who would have thought?"

"I know." He said with a smile. "So I am banished to this island until the two of us figure out a way off of it without magic."

Tara wasn't sure what to say to that so she just walked away.

Chapter Three

Tara didn't know how long they would be on the island but she knew they needed some kind of a plan. She decided to look around for food. It wasn't long before she saw a banana tree up ahead. She looked around and saw some branches, which was odd but she didn't complain because somebody was looking out for her. So she grabbed a tree branch and started throwing it up, hoping to knock some bananas down. She threw the branch up and it came crashing down and hit her in the back. "Ow. That hurt." She yelled. She threw it up again and it missed the tree completely. "Ugh." She stomped her foot into the stand. Not giving up, she threw it up there until she knocked a couple down figuring they could always come back later for more.

Proud of herself Tara picked up the bananas with a big smile on her face and started walking back to Mark. When she made it back to him she handed him one. "Here. I got dinner."

He took one from her. "Thanks. That was nice of you."

She walked over kicked at the sand as if she was making a spot to sit perfect and then sat down. "You're welcome. Now what's the plan? How do we get off this island?"

Mark let out a sigh as he peeled his banana. "I have no idea. Before today if I wanted something I would just snap my fingers or point or whatever and there you go."

Tara smiled. "Yeah I know. Shoes on fire."

Mark looked over at her and raised his eyebrow. "Really? Rub it in much? I get it. I messed up."

"Well I didn't ask to be here." Tara said. "One minute I'm cleaning out my grandma's attic and the next minute you show up and become a huge pain in my ass."

"Well that isn't usually how people thank me." He said.

"Thank You. Thank You? You have got to be joking." Tara stood up ready to fight. She was pacing back and forth. "You forced me to make wishes that I didn't want and then when I did you played with the words and ruined them. You dropped an ice truck in my driveway. You lit my shoes on fire. Oh that was so much fun."

Mark was laughing. "That was a little funny. I mean come on that was a little funny."

"Then you ship me off here to this island"

"Now wait." Mark said. "You asked to be left alone. That is exactly what I did." He laughed at that even more.

Tara couldn't hold the tears back as they poured down her face. "Sure laugh. Why not? It's all fun and games for you. Well for me I have had a horrible week. I lost my grandma. I had her funeral. I was trying to clean out her attic when I found you the very next day. Then I had to deal with all your crap. I had to take care of all of the things she promised people because she wouldn't have wanted to be an imposition to anyone. She was a really wonderful person. She raised me when my parents died. But you know what you don't care about any of this you got to have fun and torment me for a week." Tara wiped the tears from her face and walked off.

Mark sat there, not saying much. He looked across the water and yelled to the head Genie. "She has had enough. Leave me here. Don't punish her for my mistakes. Let her go and leave me here."

Tara walked around for a awhile trying to avoid Mark, not really knowing what to do. She was trapped on an island with a guy who used to be a genie of all things. It was something that would be in a fairytale and not real life. The sad part of it all was that she wasn't in a huge hurry to get off the island because she had nowhere to go and no one to go home to. She had acquaintances but nobody to call a true friend. The only thing waiting for her was a lonely life. As she walked around she looked for a place that might be a good sleeping place but nothing really looked like it would work and the sun was starting to set so she headed back to where she left Mark.

When she walked back to where Mark was she found him building a fire. She looked over at him. "Hi. I'm back."

"Hi. Sorry but I kind of looked through your purse and found some matches. I used them to start a fire."

Tara nodded. "Sure. No problem. I don't smoke. Somebody was passing them out one day with some advertisement on them. I guess they came in handy after all." She smiled. "Plus, I don't think I will need my purse anyway if I'm never getting off this island."

Mark frowned and went over to her. He touched her arm gently. "I am so sorry Tara. I was a jerk. This is all my fault. I was mad and frustrated with my life and I took it out on you and that wasn't fair to you and now you are stuck here on this island instead of living your life where you should be. I'm going to do everything I can to get you off here. First thing tomorrow I will build a raft or something."

Tara laughed. "Out of what? She laughed even harder. "Don't worry about it. Really. My life isn't that great anyway. My grandma was the only good thing in it and now she is gone. So I don't have anybody to rush home to anyway. Nobody is waiting for me or worrying about me."

Mark took her hand and led her over to the fire. As they sat down he said. "Well my life has been one big mistake after another lately. I've been a genie my whole life. But after a while it gets old you know. I mean people are so greedy. It's nothing but I want. I want. Give me this. Give me that. So I said that's it. I'm done. No more. I don't want to be a genie anymore. I want out. I asked if I could be done and I was told no. So I asked for a vacation and again I was told no. So I started being the evil genie and that was fun." He said with a smile.

Tara picked up a stick and stirred the fire. "Well you must have done something to my grandma because she had a note on your lamp that said don't make a wish. I thought she was just joking but she must have made a wish and you must have been mean to her."

Mark looked away in shame. "I'm so sorry. I wish I could take it back."

Tara could see it in his eyes that he truly felt sorry. "It couldn't have been that bad. She never talked about it. I'm sure it was a harmless prank."

"It doesn't make me feel any better about myself though." Mark said. " I know it's not going to be very comfortable but let's try and get some sleep tonight here on the sand and in the morning we will start looking for food and shelter and maybe something to build a raft out of. I don't know I'm just brainstorming ideas. I'm not even sure if we can find anything to build stuff out of but we have to at least look."

Tara shook her ahead. "I agree. Not much else we can do. Might as well lay here in front of the fire. It's as good a place as any." She lay down in front of the fire on the sand with no pillow, blanket or bed.

Chapter Four

The sun hit Tara in the face waking her up immediately as she rolled over. She didn't see Mark at first. She jumped up looking around to find him hoping he wasn't gone as she didn't want to be left all alone. She felt her heart starting to beat faster in fear. Off in a distant she saw him walking toward her with something in his hands. She let out the breath she had been unknowingly holding.

Mark walked up to Tara with his arms full of coconuts and bananas. "Good morning. I didn't want to wake you so I went and got us some breakfast. I'll crack these coconuts for the milk and here are some bananas."

Tara walked over and took the bananas from him. "Thanks. I thought you left me. I'm so glad you came back." She looked away quickly."

Mark looked over at her and was starting to feel something for her. "I wouldn't leave you." He said softly. Then he cracked the coconut on the rock. "Here you're probably thirsty." He handed it to her.

"Thanks." She took a sip and thought it did feel pretty nice having something to drink.

Tara pushed her hair out of her face and looked out at the water. "It's beautiful here, but what are we supposed to do? I mean sure we could just stay here forever eating bananas." She laughed. "But seriously how long do you think they are going to punish you? And when they remove your punishment will they take me home too? Not that I really have anything to go home to, but I don't want to be here all alone either."

Mark walked over to her and sat down beside her. "I'm so sorry I did this to you. I promise you I won't leave you. If they lift my punishment I will make this right. I won't leave you here alone. I promise."

Tara looked up in his eyes and could see how genuine he was. She didn't know why but she was starting to fall for him. First she hated him but the longer she was with him the closer she was drawn to him. *Was that part of the Head Genie's plan? Were they matchmakers? She thought to herself.* "Okay. Well since we have no idea when or if that will ever happen why don't we spend the day exploring this island for some kind of shelter and some kind of food other than bananas." She tossed the peel into the fire as they started to explore.

As they were walking they heard the sound of water falling. "Maybe that is fresh water that we can drink." Tara said. "Let's go see."

Mark reached out for her. "Hold on. Be careful. You don't know what's up ahead."

Tara laughed. "Yes I do."

"What do you mean?" Mark asked completely confused.

Tara smiled at him. "I wished to be left all alone and you granted me that wish and you gave me exactly what I wished for right? So there is nothing at all on this island that could harm me because there is nothing on this island."

Mark couldn't help but laugh. "Good point. Well at least be careful not to fall then. At least let me say that." He laughed.

Tara walked on up the path with Mark following close behind. When they got to the end of the path was a beautiful pool of water that an amazing waterfall of fresh water drained into. Tara looked around and the tropical trees that gave just enough shading but left the perfect amount of

sunlight. "It's beautiful. We can swim here."
She pointed. "And drink from the waterfall."
She pointed over there. "We will still look
for some fruits and things too to eat but we
are at least getting a start."

Mark watched at how excited she
was. "Yeah. It's great. We'll find
somewhere to sleep close by here that way
we don't have to walk so far each day. There
should be something close by to make some
shelter."

"Sounds good." Tara agreed.

They walked around for a little while
looking for somewhere that would make a
good bed. Tara couldn't help but think it
really was a beautiful island it hadn't been
that horrible of a time being there with Mark
either. She was actually enjoying herself as
crazy as that was. *Is it sad that my life is
actually better on a deserted island with a
guy who didn't really like me much until he
was stuck here with me?* She thought to
herself. She was pulled out of her thoughts
by the sound of Mark calling for her.

'Tara. I found the perfect place."

Tara turned and started walking in
the direction of his voice. When she made it
around the trees she found a small cave area.
It wasn't big but it would work. They could

sleep in it and at least stay out of the weather. It was a nice island so cold weather wasn't going to be an issue, but it could always rain and it would be nice to not be woken up by water falling down on her head. "It's perfect. Too bad we don't have a bed in there and some pillows." She laughed.

Marked laughed. "Too bad I don't have my powers. I would have us some instantly." Then his smile faded. "I'm sorry. This is all my fault. You didn't ask for any of this."

Tara walked over to him and put her hand on his the side of his face gently. "Mark, it's fine. Really. It's actually been kind of fun. I wouldn't want to be here with anyone else."

Mark leaned down and kissed her softly. Then he stepped back. "Okay. We need food."

Tara was a little surprised by the kiss but she liked it. "Yeah. I'm hungry but I really don't want another banana. So is there a pizza place close by?"

Mark laughed. "Okay, we can try to spear a fish. That would be a good dinner."

Tara couldn't help but laugh. She held her stomach as she laughed so hard.

"Well that would be nice but if you saw how hard it was for me to get the bananas earlier you wouldn't suggest that. I hit myself with the stick more times than I did the bananas. I don't see how we will ever actually get a fish without your magic."

Mark determined to prove his manhood. "Oh please. It can't be that hard to catch a fish. Let's start with a long stick and then stab at it. Or spear at it or, I don't know, chase it out of the water."

Tara was laughing so hard she couldn't even talk. "So you want us to run around scaring the fish out of the water. I don't think that is going to work out for us. Maybe we can figure something else out. Maybe we can find some berries or something or just suck it up and eat another banana. At least we know we can get those out of the tree. Or maybe your bosses will just feel sorry for us and drop a steak dinner down by airplane. I mean, just because they are punishing you, why would they punish me? I didn't do anything."

Mark looked at her with one of his okay that's enough looks.

Tara smiled. "What. I'm just saying. Surely they have to feel sorry for me. I didn't do anything." She laughed as she sat there twirling a stick in her hand.

Mark started walking towards the water. "Come on." He glanced over his shoulder with a smile. "Let's go try and scare up some food."

Tara hurried along to catch up with him.

When they walked out of the path and onto the beach they saw a table set up with two chairs. As they got closer to it they saw that what looked like a dinner for two. A bottle of wine sat chilling in a bucket. Two plates covered with silver lid as if they were at a fancy restaurant. When Tara took the lid off she saw a steak dinner. She couldn't help but laugh.

"Oh my God. You have got to be kidding me."

"What is it?" Mark hurried to her side.

"It is my steak dinner. That is exactly what it is. It is a steak and baked potato, roll, wine. A dinner for two." She laughed. "You are in trouble. But they are watching out for us. I asked for a steak dinner and they gave us exactly that. This is too funny."

Mark didn't find it as funny as Tara but he did walk over to the table. "Okay I'll eat the dinner. Of course. I'm no idiot. But I don't understand what is going on."

"Who cares?" Tara said with a mouthful of food. "We are here. I have nothing better to do. So If I'm part of the plan to help you be a better you and I get a free steak dinner in the process and a vacation on a beautiful island so be it." She laughed. "And I get a not too hard on the eyes tour guide on top of that. So it's win-win for me."

"Well I'm glad you are enjoying yourself." He smiled as he tossed a roll at her.

"So let's eat before the food gets cold." Tara said as she started cutting her steak.

Mark took a bite but he sat there with a confused troubled look on his face. "I don't understand this. So all day yesterday they made us take care of ourselves. Then today you ask for a steak dinner and get one. What is the point to all of this? How long are we supposed to stay here? Not that I'm complaining about that part." He said as he looked over at her and smiled. "I mean really I could stay here with you forever. But, I'm just saying, what is the end game to all of this?"

Tara shrugged her shoulders. "I have no clue. I have never been the pawn in the middle of a genie chess game before."

Mark reached over the table and touched her hand. "Yes. I am so sorry about all of this, but at least the head genies are trying to give you something in return to at least make up for it a little bit although I don't know why they don't just send you home and wipe your memory or something."

Tara's face suddenly froze. "What! No! They can't!" She stood up. "I don't want that to happen. I don't want to forget you. Don't let them take you away from me."

Mark went over to her and pulled her into his chest. "I'm sorry. I didn't mean to upset you. I won't let that happen."

Tara snuggled in close to him. "I know we haven't known each other long and we had a rocky start to say the least but I don't know what I would do without you. I've never met anyone like you. I need you."

Mark held her tighter. "I won't leave you Tara. I promise." Then he tried to lighten the mood. "Besides, it looks like we are stuck on this island anyway."

Tara laughed. "So you are stuck with me whether you like it or not is what you are saying."

Mark smiled. "Yep pretty much now let's finish this awesome meal."

Tara finished her dinner and looked around.

Mark stood up and looked around trying to figure out what she was doing. "What are you looking for?"

"Well. We have dirty dishes and scraps and things. We need to clean up the mess. I don't have anywhere to do that. We can't just leave this stuff here and we can't wash the dishes in the clean water we are going to drink. We don't want to litter up the ocean water with dirty dishes. Then the scraps of food will destroy this beautiful island and I don't want that even if it is make-believe; because I am not one hundred percent sure if it is real or not. I don't know what to do."

Before Mark could answer her everything vanished before their eyes.

"Well, okay then." Tara said. "We can always go with that route with it too." She looked around. "What happened to everything?"

"I don't know." Mark said. "But I think something strange is going on.

Tara glanced over her shoulder and back to Mark. "I think so too. When I went to get bananas earlier I couldn't reach them. I looked around for something and then all of the sudden there were branches there. But the only trees around were Palm trees. They don't have branches."

Mark got up and looked around. "It's my boss."

Tara jumped up. "What?"

"It's got to be. How else can you explain this?" I'm being punished but they don't want to punish you."

Chapter Five

Tara and Mark had walked to the cave where they planned to sleep. Neither said much on the walk. Tara was still a little confused from the events of the night. As they got to the cave's entrance and started in she turned to Mark. "If your boss is keeping an eye on us then what is the point of all of this? I mean why did he or she or whatever make us go look for food to begin with? Why didn't they just have a big box of supplies waiting when we got here? It doesn't make much sense."

Mark shook his head. "I guess I hadn't earned it. Or you hadn't asked. I don't know."

Tara sat there for a minute thinking. "Well if all I have to do is ask then maybe I can ask for us to be let off the island but." She stopped and sadness took over her face.

Mark walked over to her. "What is it?"

She looked up at him and slowly started to talk. "Is this all make-believe or some crazy dream. I mean what happens when we are off the island? Where do you go? Where do I go? Can we have a relationship? Do you even want one with me? Do I go back to my grandma's big old empty house and live my lonely life? I don't know that I do want to ask them to end this all."

Mark suddenly understood exactly what she meant. "I see what you mean. I don't know. I don't want to lose you either. I don't want to go back to my old life and I don't want you to go back to yours but obviously we can't just stay on an island with just the two of us forever so you are going to have to end this and apparently they will listen to you. They made that clear with the steak dinner. So you are going to have to call them down here to talk to us so we can figure this out."

Tara was very nervous about it and wasn't sure she was going to like the answer but she knew she had to do it. "Excuse me. I hate to interrupt, but Mark's Boss, I'm sorry I don't know your name. When you have a minute, can we talk?"

It seemed like a few minutes went by and Tara saw what looked like a falling star shooting across the sky and coming right toward the island. It was getting closer and closer until it landed in the sand in front of her. Then a beautiful woman with long brown hair appeared in the light. "You wanted to talk. And you can call me Miranda."

"Yes." Tara said. "I'm so sorry for all the trouble Mark caused and he is sorry too. He has changed and he will never act like that again. We have a few things we would like to ask."

"What is it?" The woman asked.

Tara nervously asked. "Is there any way at all that you could see fit to let Mark and me off the island? And let Mark be a human and live a normal life? Because I think I've fallen in love with him." She glanced over at Mark to see if he was looking at her.

The Head Genie smiled at them. "I knew you were good for him."

Tara was confused. "I'm sorry. What?"

The Head Genie looked over at Mark. "Mark, is this you want? And will you take care of her?"

"Yes Ma'am. I love her."

Tara stepped up. "What do you mean; you knew I was good for him? How do you know me?"

The Head Genie smiled down at Tara. "I've watched over you for many years. Your mother was one of my very best friends. I made sure that Mark's lamp made it into your house at one time but your grandma ended up finding it instead and let's just say Mark wasn't very nice to her." She glanced over at Mark and then back to Tara. "I knew once the two of you got together you would be perfect for each other."

Tara didn't know what to say. She stood there taking it all in trying to wrap her head around the fact that her mother was best friends with a genie. Secondly she was destined to be with a genie. After what seemed like an eternity of silence but was just a few seconds she finally spoke. "I don't know what to say exactly. That is a lot of stuff to take in all at once. But I do want to thank you for everything. For watching over me. For not leaving us stranded on the island and for the lovely dinner." She was starting to ramble.

The Head Genie interrupted her. "Let me ask the two of you again. Is this what you both want? You both want off the island and to be together as humans?"

They both nodded their heads.

"Then I'll grant your wish. I will send you both back home and since you have learned your lesson I will give you all your powers back. You do not have to live your life as a mortal human. Just behave yourself from now on." With that she disappeared.

The next minute Tara and Mark were back in the living room of Tara's grandma's house.

Tara put her arms around Mark. "You were going to give up your whole life and become a mortal for me. Nobody has ever done anything like that for me."

Mark kissed her. "Nobody has ever meant as much to me before."

The End.

A Lost Memory

Lizzy Stevens

Steve Miller

A Lost Memory

Lizzy Stevens & Steve Miller

Dedication:

We dedicate this book to Jason and Noah

Chapter One

Alley lay in bed in a strange room. Glancing around nothing was familiar. *Where was she?* She sat up, a tingle creeping up her spine. *What was going on?* Anxious to get out of there, Alley yanked away the blanket and stood. Pain shot through her head, threatening to blow it apart. Her finger pressed her temple instinctively to ease the pain. She felt a bandage taped to her forehead. *What has happened to me? Where am I?* No longer able to withstand the pain, she lay back down.

Drifting off to sleep, images of a young man filled her dreams. She didn't recognize him, but he was handsome with six pack abs and long sandy blonde hair that brushed the top of his shoulders. *But who was he?*

Alley come back to me. The man seemed to know her, but she didn't recognize him at all.

Alley was awakened by the sound of the door opening. She saw a woman standing in the doorway holding a ceramic bowl of water.

"Oh, sweetie! You're awake," the woman said as tears rolled down her face. She wiped at them as she walked over to the bed.

Alley stared at her not knowing what to say. *Am I supposed to know this woman?*

"Oh, Alley, I know you're confused, honey. It's me, Mom."

Alley glanced around the room for answers but none came to her. "Mom?" she asked, puzzled.

"Yes dear, you've been in a terrible accident and the doctor warned us that your memory may be fuzzy when you came to."

"An accident? What kind of accident?" Alley didn't understand anything at that moment. She didn't remember any accident.

"Honey, don't push yourself to remember right now. We'll talk about this later. I need to call your doctor and get him over here to examine you at once." She turned and hurried out of the room.

Alley sat there more confused than she was before. She hoped the doctor would be able to shed some light on what was going on.

She glanced around the room and saw an antique dresser with three drawers made from mahogany. In the corner stood a full length mirror. The four-poster bed where she lay was draped in a sheer white canopy. Beside the bed was a small table where her mother placed the ceramic bowl of water. In the opposite corner sat a rocking chair with a red and white quilt folded neatly over the back. Everything looked neat and well taken care of, but none of it looked familiar.

* * *

A while later there was a knock at her door.

"Come in," Alley called from across the room.

The woman who claimed to be her mother was standing there with a man in a white lab coat.

"Alley this is Doctor Monroe." she said as they walked closer to the bed.

Doctor Monroe carried his black medical bag and set it on the bed beside Alley. He removed the stethoscope to give

Alley a thorough examination. He checked her heartbeat, pulse and blood pressure. Then he moved onto the bandage on her head. "Everything looks good Alley. I'm going to redress your wound and give you some pain medicine to help with the swelling."

"Doctor, I don't know who I am. I can't remember anything. I don't even recognize my own mother. What happened to me? What kind of accident was I in?"

Alley watched Doctor Monroe glanced up at her mother who gave a slight shake of her head.

"Alley, these things take time. Don't bother yourself with all of these details right now. You've been in a coma for a week. We don't want to overload your brain with all these details. Your memory will come back in time, and if it doesn't then we will cross that bridge when we get to it. For now I want you to take it easy. Get lots of rest and when you're feeling better take a walk. It's beautiful this time of the year and the fresh air will do you good."

Alley was more confused than ever

now. She thought that seeing the doctor would help her figure out who she was and what was going on, but instead he was no help at all. *What are they hiding? I've been in a coma for a week, but I'm not in a hospital?*

She watched as her mother walked the doctor to the door.

When the doctor walked out, Alley said, "Mom, help me remember."

Her mother approached, a worried expression on her face. She fidgeted with a string on her shirt avoiding Alley's eyes. "Alley, you heard the doctor. We can't push you."

"I know, Mom, but I want to know at least a few things about myself like what is my full name? For that matter, what is your name? Where do we live? What month is it? What year is it?"

"Alley, slow down, honey. You're going so fast that I can't keep up." Her mom chuckled. "Okay, I'll help you a little, but we can't overdo it. Your name is Allison Marie Anderson. You prefer Alley. My name is Catherine Anderson. Its springtime and the month of April." Catherine reached out for her daughter's hand. "The doctor's right, it's beautiful this time of the year. When you're up to it we'll get outside and maybe something will jog your memory. As for the year it's 2012, and we live in a small town called Rock City. Now, I really think you should get some rest. We don't want to push you too fast."

"Okay. Thank you for filling in some of the blanks. My head is throbbing. I'm going to rest a little bit."

Catherine leaned down and kissed her daughter's forehead, pulled the blankets up to her chin and turned the lamp off beside the bed. She turned and blew Alley a kiss as she exited the room.

Alley quickly drifted off to sleep, but it wasn't long before dream man re-appeared. Winter snow blanketed the ground.. She rode on the back of his sled going downhill after hill. She was laughing and had her arms wrapped around him. She was happy. At the bottom of the last hill he faced her, gently kissing her on the lips. They rolled off the sled, the man grabbed the rope and they started back up the hill to go again. Dream man put his arm around Alley as she snuggled in closer to him. She could see the love in his eyes. *Who was he?* The dreams felt so real.

Alley come back to me. She heard him calling her. It wasn't a dream. She could hear him plain as day, but it faded until she could hear it no more.

"Who are you? How do you know me?" Alley called out in her sleep, but got no answer in return.

Alley's eyes popped open to an empty room. Nobody was around and her dream man must be just that-- a dream. *But why do I keep dreaming about the same man? Where have I seen him before? Maybe Mom knows.*

* * *

The next morning Alley decided it was time to get out of bed and try to get her life back. She still had no memory of anything, but she intended to change that.

She followed the smell of bacon and eggs down a spiral staircase with a dark cherry wood hand rail. As she got to the end of the stairs she stepped onto hardwood floors waxed to a perfect shine. The house was beautiful but looked like it was very old. She followed the smell to the kitchen where she found her mother standing at a mahogany table cutting fruit for a platter.

"Good morning, Mother."

Catherine jumped. "Alley, you startled me. Honey, you shouldn't be up walking around yet."

"I'm fine, Mom. I want to get back to my life. I want to do just as the doctor said. I plan to explore outside today. I may need a little direction before I get started." She huffed out a short laugh.

Her mother grinned at her as she finished slicing fruits. Alley admired the ripe, juicy strawberries, kiwi, and grapes. Her stomach growled.

Catherine set the table and poured Alley a glass of orange juice to go with her breakfast.

As Alley sat down she turned to her mother. "Mother. How old am I?"

"Alley don't worry so much. Your memory will come back, and if it doesn't you'll be fine. Head injuries are unpredictable, but to answer your question you're twenty–two."

Alley ate her breakfast as more

and more questions popped into her head. There was so much that she wanted and needed to know. "Where is my father? Do I have a father?"

"Yes, dear, you have a father. He's away on business and will return next week. He's overjoyed that you're awake and can't wait to see you."

"Mom...thanks for putting up with all my questions. I'm trying to remember. I want to remember. I feel like there's a big piece missing from me. I don't feel whole right now." Tears welled in her eyes and slipped down her cheeks. She wiped them away and glanced out the window. The sun was shining bright. "I'm going to go for a walk. I think it will do me good to get out."

Catherine bit her bottom lip nervously. "Okay honey, if you're sure, but be careful. You don't know your way around yet. If you get turned around follow the fence. It'll bring you back home. All four thousand acres of our land is fenced in. So if you get lost just follow the fence. It might be a long walk, but it'll get you back to the house."

Alley walked outside for the first

time. She really had no clue where she was going, but she had to try and get her memory back. She wanted to know who the man was that she kept dreaming about. *What did it all mean?*

As she walked away from the house she glanced over her shoulder. Behind her stood her home, she guessed, a beautiful white Victorian two story house with maroon trim. It had a wraparound porch with tall white columns. On the porch was a wooden swing with a maroon cushion. It swayed in the breeze, and she wondered if it was one of her favorite things to do. She was learning everything all over again.

Alley walked across the open field, drawn to the small creek. It babbled through a shady spot, courtesy of some big oak trees, with a large rock off to the side. She climbed the rock and enjoyed the cool breeze against her cheeks.

Alley, come back to me.

Alley jumped and glanced around. Nobody was there. The wind must be playing tricks on her.

Sitting by the creek watching the water flow downstream, Alley wondered who she was. The wind blew through her hair and the sun warmed her face. Alley brushed the hair away from her eyes as she lay back on the rock. She drifted off to sleep under the warmth of the sun.

Images of a winged horse as white as snow entered her mind. It was the most beautiful animal she had ever seen. It pranced in a field of wild flowers. As Alley watched, a noise startled the majestic animal and it spread its wings wide flying off into the horizon. The scene struck her as familiar. She couldn't quite put her finger on it, but she felt like she knew the place and the animal. *Angel. Yes that's it, but why do I know the name of an imaginary animal?* Head injuries were very odd. Nothing made sense anymore.

A noise off in the distance woke Alley from her dreams. Rising from the rock, she scanned the open field. No winged horse to be found. *Did I really think there would be? That's crazy. They don't even exist. My mind is simply dreaming to help it heal.*

It was getting late so Alley decided to walk back. As she approached the house she heard voices.

"You have to face the facts. Her memory may never come back," Catherine said.

"It may never come back as long as she is here. She has to come back to Majestic Falls." A man's voice said.

"That's out of the question."

"Catherine, you can't keep her here under false pretenses. Her place is with me. I know you think you're protecting her and in some ways you might be, but she has to come back home. Her people need her."

Alley had no idea what they were talking about or who the man was. In her eagerness to see him, she clumsily knocked over a flower pot that went crashing down the steps.

Catherine came running out, but she was alone.

"Is somebody here, Mother?"

"No, Sweetie. I had the radio on in the other room. Nobody is here."

Why would her mother lie? She'd heard two people having a conversation. People don't have conversations with the radio, but she knew there must be a reason that her mother didn't want to discuss it. Alley ran from room to room looking, but found nobody else in the house.

Alley needed to be alone. She went up to her room to escape into a nice hot bubble bath which she thought would help her relax. Maybe being alone with her thoughts would help her figure something out. She didn't care what, but she wanted to at least remember one thing.

She sank down into the hot steaming water letting it warm her entire body. Alley laid back and closed her eyes hoping to see the man she kept dreaming about, but he didn't appear. Sadness came over her. There was something about the guy of her dreams. She felt like she knew him.

Chapter Two

Alley walked downstairs but didn't hear anybody. She went into the kitchen but didn't find her mother where she usually was. Fear crept up in her a little. She felt alone and panic threatened. She rubbed her sweaty palms on her blue jeans. Movement from outside the window caught her eye.

Alley stepped to the backdoor to look out. She saw her mother on the sidewalk talking to somebody she didn't recognize...but then that was nothing new.

Alley walked out to find out who he was. "Hi, Mom."

Hi, honey. I'll be in to fix breakfast in just a few minutes. We were just enjoying the fresh air."

Alley was confused.

"Oh Alley, I'm sorry. This is your father."

"Dad? I'm glad you're back. I have so many questions. I hope you can help me."

"Slow down, honey. I know this has been hard for you." He walked over and put his arm around her "Don't overdo it. Let's go inside for breakfast and we can talk."

Alley joined her parents in the kitchen. She turned to her mother. "Mom, do I cook?"

Catherine smiled. "If you want to cook I can teach you a few things. It will be fun."

Alley spent the next hour in the kitchen with her mother learning to chop bell peppers and onions, peel potatoes. She fried potatoes, scrambled eggs, made fresh squeezed orange juice. Alley smiled the entire time she worked. Everything was a new experience.

As she was setting the table she turned to her father. "Dad. What's your name?"

"Mathew."

"What do you do for a living? Mother said you were away on business."

"Oh, well I…"

"That's enough talk for now." Catherine interrupted. "Let's eat."

The three of them ate their breakfast in silence as more of Alley's questions were left unanswered.

After breakfast Alley helped clean

up the dishes and the kitchen. When everything was back in order, she decided to take a walk to clear her mind. She strode down by the creek she had found before.

Alley slipped her shoes and socks off and sank her feet down into the cool water. The water flowing over her bare feet felt good. She glanced around her surroundings trying to force some small memory into her empty mind, but nothing came to her. She kicked at the water. How can I not know who I am?

Come back to me Alley.

Alley jumped up and looked around. Nobody was there. She knew she heard the voice, but couldn't figure out who it was or where it came from. *It had to mean something. She ran around in circles looking for any sign of anyone, but nothing was there. Am I losing my mind?*

Unable to solve the problem of the mysterious voice Alley sat back down on the warm rock. Soon she relaxed and lay back staring at the sky. After a few hours of soaking up the sunlight, Alley decided to head back to the house to sit down with a good book. Maybe the relaxation would help her memory. As she walked back to the house the sun was setting and the air was starting to chill.

Entering her bedroom, she walked over to the full length mirror and stared at a reflection she didn't recognize. *Who was this woman staring back at her?*

As she stared at the mirror she watched it shimmer in the light. It was as if the mirror had moved, but that wasn't possible. Her eyes must have played tricks on her. She knew that mirrors didn't move. Not really knowing what she expected to happen, Alley walked over and touched the mirror. Nothing happened. Alley glanced around the room quickly as if checking to make sure nobody saw her making a fool of herself.

Alley went to the bathroom to draw her bath. She filled it to the rim with steamy hot water and poured in a capful of tropical shea butter bubble bath. She sank down into the water and let all her worries disappear.

She stayed in the water until it turned chilly cold forcing her to get out. She wrapped up in the fluffy blue and yellow bath sheet, and then ran a brush through her wet hair. After getting dressed in her nightgown, Alley went into her room and got comfy in her four poster bed with her purple and pink down comforter. She rolled up in the blanket until she felt safe and secure and then drifted off to sleep.

Alley., I love you. Come back to me. Please. I need you.

Alley's dreams were filled with voices from her mystery man. She had to find out more about him. Maybe it meant something. How could he be a figment of her imagination? He seemed so real.

Alley found herself in a field of wild flowers. A field of yellow, pinks, greens, purples. It was beautiful. As she strolled through the open land, she saw the white winged horse off in the distance.

"Angel." She called out.

The animal swung its regal head to face Alley, and then trotted towards her.

Alley approached and put her hand out for Angel to come to her.

As the mythical creature came to her and nuzzled her hand, she rubbed its head. "Hi there. How do I know you? I wish you could talk. I need answers. I know this is a dream, but I feel so at home in my dreams. I 'm so lost when I'm awake." Alley was talking to an imaginary creature. She didn't understand why her dreams felt so real, but she found comfort with Angel.

She tossed and turned in her bed, restlessly falling in and out of her dreams. She tugged at the covers and tried to snuggle in deeper. She drifted back off to sleep after pounding her pillow hoping to get more comfortable.

Succumbing to slumber once again, Alley found herself at a waterfall in a green forest, the sun shining through the trees. Movement in the distance grabbed her attention. Her mystery man... She ran to him. Solving his identity was critical to her recovery, she just knew it. But the closer she got to him, the further he slipped away. He remained just out of reach. Alley knew that if she could only talk to him for a minute that things would get clear for her.

***

Days went by and still Alley experienced no return of her memory. Growing bored and restless, she knew that she couldn't sit around and do nothing. She had to figure out her next step. She needed to find a job and make some kind of life for herself. She'd lost her memory and she had to accept that.

Maybe she could find something in the want ads in the paper. Now that she had somewhat of a plan, Alley felt better. She got dressed and walked down the stairs. She heard her parents talking in the kitchen. Alley sat down at the bottom of the stairs to listen.

"Catherine, she isn't getting better. We have to take her back. Maybe seeing everything will jog her memory."

"No! I told Evan no, and I'm telling you no. She's not leaving. This is her only chance for a normal- mortal life."

Alley's head was spinning. *What was her mother talking about?*

"Catherine, you're being unreasonable. Majestic Falls is our home. None of this is real. Evan loves her and the people love her. She is their queen. We need to do everything we can to help her recovery her memory."

Alley didn't understand any of this. She jumped up and quickly ran back upstairs. *What is going on? What is he talking about? Am I still dreaming?* She pinched her arm to make sure. "Ouch. No, I'm not dreaming."

She had to get to the bottom of all this strangeness. She needed to know what her father was talking about. Alley had too many unanswered questions swirling around in her head.

Alley glanced at the mirror. Before her eyes the mirror shimmered as if made of water and instead of her reflection she saw herself walking with her dream man. He had his arm around her and they were walking down the path to the waterfall. Again that feeling of deja vu. Memory tugged at her but she was unable to grasp it. *This all meant something. But what?*

The vision in the mirror faded and her reflection reappeared. The mirror went back to normal and Alley's hand started to tremble. She tried to steady the shaking with her other hand but it wasn't working very well. Alley ran her hands through her hair and glanced around the room desperate for answers.

Chapter Three

The next morning Alley exited the back door for the morning walk that was becoming her daily routine. She'd become extremely restless with her lack of ability to recover her memory, and she knew she couldn't stay at the farm house day after day doing nothing with her life. She knew in her heart that something important about whom she'd been was missing, but she was going to have to figure out a way to live without it.

Alley stepped to the edge of the creek, took her shoes and socks off and dangled her feet in the cool water. As she sat there with water flowing over her feet and the warm breeze blowing through her hair, an eeriness crept down her spine. She wasn't alone.

Alley glanced around in all directions but didn't see anything or anybody. The trees were full of birds and squirrels that could have given her the sensation of being watched, but it was unlikely. After a few seconds she dismissed her worries and told herself that it was nothing.

She let her head fall back and enjoyed the feel of the warm sun on her face. Her mind wandered and was soon consumed with thoughts of the man in her dreams.

He rode up to her on a shiny horse with hair as black as coal. He jumped down from the animal with a dozen pink roses in hand.

Alley observed him as he approached and leaned down and placed a kiss on her lips, pressing the flowers into her hands.

A noise in the distance woke Alley from her thoughts. Determination filled her. She would find out who he was.

Alley strolled the acreage for a few more hours. It was an odd place. As she followed the fence line butterflies seemed to be attracted to her. Yellow and blue butterflies with black spots followed her as she walked. They seemed to be accompanying her, but she knew that was impossible. The logical reason would be that they were attracted to the scent of her soap, shampoo or deodorant. *Butterflies couldn't know a person or follow a person. Could they?* Alley held her finger out to watch what would happen. Before her very eyes one of them landed on her finger. She stared at it in awe. After a few seconds the creature flew away, followed by its companions.

She observed them until the last one disappeared. More confused than ever, she returned to the house.

* * *

Frustration filled Alley after spending days with no memory gain. Her mind was now full of her dreams which weren't real, yet she suspected they must be clues to some part of her life. Nothing made sense. Her world was upside down and she didn't know how to set it right.

Alone she strolled back to her favorite spot by the creek. It reminded her of the waterfall of her dreams. As she got closer she saw somebody standing there.

The man of her dreams turned to face her. Recognition was instantaneous. The flash of memory returning staggered her. "Evan? It's you. It's really you."

Evan ran to her and put his arms

around her. "Oh Alley, you came back to me."

"I can't believe this. I remember. I remember you. I remember us. I remember Majestic Falls. Oh my God. Majestic Falls. We have to get back there. Esmeralda...."

Evan leaned down and kissed her gently on the lips. His hands traced her face then threaded through her hair. He pressed her against him. "I missed you so much Alley. You are my whole world."

"I missed you too Evan. I was lost without you, but we must get back to Majestic Falls at once." She stepped back abruptly. "We can't let Esmeralda take over our land. We must fight her."

"Slow down, Alley. Slow down a minute. Don't overdo it."

"I'm fine. Really. My memory is back, and I want to get home."

Evan raked a hand through his hair. He felt a little uneasy about Alley wanting to go fight a battle so quickly. He agreed that she needed to come home. He needed her with him, but he didn't want her to get hurt. "Alley, what happened? Nobody saw anything or knew anything.

You were found in the meadow unconscious with a cut on your head. What happened?"

"Esmeralda happened. She came to the meadow and we had words. Then it escalated into a full blown argument. She said she would have our land and she would be the new Queen of Majestic Falls. I said over my dead body. Before I knew it she had twenty of her men right in front of me." Alley paced the grassy meadow her fingers pressed to her temples.

"All I remember is one of them swinging their sword and it hitting me in the head. Before they could do anything else, I fell to the ground hitting my head on a big rock. Something must have scared them off. I found the bandage on my head when I woke up at the farm house. How I got there is still a little fuzzy."

"Alley, I'm sorry about all of this. Esmeralda wouldn't have this vengeance against you and Majestic Falls if I hadn't hurt her the way I did. She is hurting you to get back at me."

"Evan this isn't your fault. You and I fell in love. It was destiny. You weren't meant to be with her. All you did was be honest with her and she is the one that couldn't handle it."

Evan pulled Alley in close to him. "Alley I'm so sorry I wasn't with you. I should have been with you."

"Evan you can't be with me all the time. I should have used my powers to stop the attack, but I was caught off guard and didn't have the time to react. Esmeralda will get what she deserves. We must get back to Majestic Falls at once."

Chapter Four

Alley and Evan walked up to her bedroom to where the mirror was.

"We need to get back now. Leave a note for my mother and father to meet us there quickly. I still need to have a talk with her about her keeping secrets from me."

"Alley, don't be so hard on her. She was trying to protect you. She didn't know if your memory would ever come back. If she told you that you live in a faraway land, you're the Queen of that land and that the farm house isn't real just an alternate universe, don't you think that would be a little hard to believe? She did the best she could, and I don't blame her for the way she handled things. Don't be angry at her. You need your family in your life."

Alley gently touched Evan's face. "That's why I love you so much. You're always my voice of reason." They stepped through the portal into Majestic Falls. Alley was finally home.

As they crossed over to the other side, Alley was greeted by pixies, fairies, elves, and animals of all kinds. The entire kingdom was excited to see her back.

As they stepped through the portal they were surrounded by servants waiting to take them back to the castle.

Alley climbed into the horse drawn carriage being pulled by two horses white as snow. She stared at the home she had missed for all those weeks seeing the damage that had happened while she was gone. As she rode through the town she witnessed burned down houses, buildings in rubble and debris everywhere. She knew Esmeralda must be the reason for all of the damage.

"Oh, everything is a mess. Esmeralda will pay for everything she's done. She will pay for the heartache she has caused the people of Majestic Falls."

Evan put his arm around Alley and pulled her in close to him.

Alley's eyes filled with tears as they rode through her beloved kingdom. "We must gather the army. We will get our revenge on her, but we must be smart about it."

The castle came into view as they rounded a corner. Upon their approach the drawbridge lowered and Alley was finally home.

She rushed to her room to take a quick look. Everything was as she'd left it. She ran her fingers across her white Oak dresser trimmed with pink flowers. It had a square mirror that reflected her room. There was a maroon sectional couch in one corner with a coffee table directly in front of it. Adjoining the sleeping area was a cozy place to have her morning tea. Everything was unchanged and perfect. She was so relieved to be back.

After Alley got settled Evan asked the chef to prepare dinner for them. "Alley, honey, I'm so glad you're back and safe with me. I won't let anything else happen to you."

Alley's lips curved and her heart swelled with love. "Thanks Evan. We have to figure out what we're going to do. The minute Esmeralda learns that I'm back she is going to be ready to fight. We must be one step ahead of her."

"I'll get Henry to come here at once and we'll lay out a plan for his army of men."

As they continued to talk, the chef

tapped on the door. He pushed the silver cart into the room and laid out their plates and glasses on the table.

Alley approached the table and poured a glass of red wine to go with their dinner. She removed the silver plate cover to see what was for dinner. She was starving.

Alley's stomach growled as she sat down to her plate of grilled chicken breast with a baked potato loaded with sour cream, chives, bits of bacon and cheddar cheese melted on top. To the side was a bowl with Caesar salad and a small plate of wheat rolls with butter and honey on a smaller plate.

As they ate Alley remained lost in thought. After they'd eaten, Alley spoke, "Evan we can't let her take over Majestic Falls. I think I have a plan."

"Alley, you can't battle her one on one. She is too powerful and dangerous."

"She's too powerful and dangerous here."

"What are you talking about?"

"Hear me out before you say anything, because I know this is a dangerous plan, but I think it will work.

Our powers are only good here in Majestic Falls. Esmeralda and I could go back and forth hurling spells at each other, or we could outsmart her. We need to get her to cross over to the other side.

Evan stood up immediately, tossed his napkin down on the table and ran his hands through his hair. "Alley that is crazy. Then what, the two of you have a fist fight? This is ridiculous."

"No, of course not. We aren't going to have a fist fight." Alley couldn't help but laugh at the thought. "We are going to outsmart her. What I want to do is trick her into following me to the other side. Her magic will be useless there.""

"Yes Alley, but so will yours." Evan interrupted.

"I know Evan, but pixie dust won't be."

Evan's eyebrows raised a little. "What are you saying?"

"I could carry a potion with me through the portal, get her to follow, throw it on her and we could destroy her forever."

"Alley this is very dangerous. How do we know that the potion will travel the portal and work on the other side?"

"We don't know for sure. That's why we need to do a test run first."

Evan's expression showed his unhappiness about the plan, but he did agree that they needed to do something. "Okay. Let's get a couple of our best men here to discuss the plan."

* * *

A few hours later Alley's butler came to her room. "Miss Alley, Mr. Thomas is here to see you."

"Thank you. Please tell Evan to meet us in the library. I'll be there in a few minutes."

Alley quickly ran a brush through her hair. She tossed the brush down on the dresser and then went to lay out her plan.

As she walked in she saw Evan and Thomas both waiting for her. "Thank you for meeting us, Thomas."

"It's my honor, my Queen. The minute I heard that you and King Evan wanted to see me I came as fast as I could."

"Can I get you a drink? Tea,

Water?"

"No thank you, Your Highness. What can I do for you?" Thomas asked his voice conveying excitement.

"Esmeralda has a done a number on Majestic Falls in my absence and this cannot go unpunished."

"I agree, Your Majesty. How can I help?"

Alley glanced over at Evan and then back to Thomas. "King Evan and I have devised a plan. Esmeralda's magic is useless in the human world. We need her to cross over so that we can attack her on the other side."

Thomas rubbed his palms on his pants nervously. His hand went to his head and scratched lightly thinking everything over before speaking. "Queen Alley? How do you plan to defeat her on the other side? If her powers are no good then yours will be no good as well. Right?"

Alley rose and fixed Thomas a cup of hot chamomile tea to settle his nerves. She handed it to him and then returned to her seat. "That is correct Thomas, but we have an idea that we need to test."

"What is it?"

"We want to test this theory of course, but the plan is to get Esmeralda to follow me into the portal and cross over to the other world. I will have a glass potion bottle in my pocket and when we get to the other side I'll throw it on her and we will be done with her. Now we all know that Esmeralda is too smart to simply stand there and let me throw a bottle on her, so the plan is to tell her that I have something for her from Evan. We know she never got over Evan so we will use that against her. She still loves him and that's how we get her. We need to see if the bottle and the magic will make it through the portal, and then see if the magic works in the human world. Then we will figure out the plan to get her to follow me."

"It's very dangerous dealing with Esmeralda, my Queen, but if this works it will be excellent news to the people of Majestic Falls. When do you want to test it?"

"Tomorrow afternoon. I need to make a couple of potions first. Come back around noon tomorrow and King Evan and I will be ready."

After Thomas left, Alley walked to Evan and snuggled into his arms. She had missed him while she was gone. Nothing made her happier than being back in his arms.

"Let's go to bed Alley."

"Now that sounds like a plan." Alley laughed as she walked hand in hand with the man of her dreams.

They walked into their bedroom and Alley turned to Evan. "I think I'd like to soak in a nice hot bubble bath before bed. Would you be interested in joining me?" She asked him slyly.

"You don't have to ask me twice." Evan followed her into the bathroom and began drawing the bath for them.

Alley walked back into the other room and poured them both a glass of wine to enjoy while soaking in the bath. When she entered the bathroom the scent of lavender and the soft light of flickering candles made her smile. Rose petals floated along the top of the water.

She handed Evan the glasses and undressed. She sat down in the hot steamy water, and Evan stepped in behind her.

Evan wrapped his arms around Alley. He moved her hair and then kissed her gently on the neck. "I missed you, Alley, and I love you more than anything in the world. "

"I missed you too Evan. I'm sorry I frightened you. We will get her though. You can count on that. We will get her. She'll pay for the hurt she's caused."

After the water turned cold, they climbed out, got in bed and snuggled in close as they both drifted off to sleep.

The next morning Alley got up excited to begin her day. "I'm going to ask my mother if she would like to help with the potions. I think it will do her some good to know she is helping and that I have no hard feelings about her wanting me to stay in the other world. She was just looking out for what she thought was best."

"That's a good idea, Honey. I need to bring your father up to date with the plan and how he can help. He is the best man in our army."

Chapter Five

Alley and Catherine spent hours making different potions and filling glass bottles. They made one set for the test run and one set for the actual showdown.

"Alley you must be careful."

"I will, Mother. She won't catch me off guard this time."

"How do you plan to get her to follow you into the portal though?"

"Don't worry I have it all planned out. This will work." Alley tried her best to reassure her mother.

The black pot simmered on the back of the stove as they took turns stirring it with a wooden spoon. One potion would freeze Esmeralda so she couldn't attack and the other was a vanishing potion that would destroy her.

Alley filled the bottles, sealed them with a wooden cork and placed them in her brown suede bag.

It was time for her to meet back up with Evan, Thomas and her father to do the test run.

Alley went up to her room and turned the candle holder that opened the hidden door. Stepping through, she followed the winding stairs to the basement where she would meet up with Evan and her father to go through the portal that was hidden there.

"Alley, is everything ready?"

"Yes. We made a couple of different potions. I'm ready to cross through."

The three of them walked through the portal and ended up in the bedroom of the farm house.

Alley looked around but nobody was there. Having the urge to double check everything, she walked over, opened the closet door but found it empty. She turned to her father and Evan. "Okay we're good. The bag made it and the potions made it. Let's go outside and throw these so Esmeralda doesn't see the broken vials when I get her to cross through."

The three of them walked down the staircase and out the door to the porch.

Alley pulled the first one out of her bag and tossed it at a large boulder in the yard. The rock exploded and disappeared, black smoke rising from the dark spot on the ground. Alley smiled and nodded.

"Okay let's get back to the castle and I'll share the plan with you on how I am going to get her to follow me."

The three of them walked back upstairs and stepped through the standing mirror. They followed the winding stairs back up to Alley's room.

"Thanks for testing this with us, Dad. We'll get with you soon about the plan."

Alley turned to Evan. "Are you hungry? I thought we might get some dinner before we work through this plan."

"Sounds good to me. " Evan said. "I'll tell the chef."

Evan went to tell the chef while Alley went onto her room to wait for him there. She wasn't feeling very well. She didn't know if it was the accident or something else. She decided to send for the doctor. She felt sick to her stomach and her head throbbed.

Evan walked back up to the room where Alley was standing with her hand on her head. "Is everything alright?"

Concern filled his voice.

"I'm okay. I don't feel well so I've sent for the doctor as a precaution. I'm sure everything is fine. Is our food about ready?"

"Yes. The chef said he would bring it in a few minutes."

As expected, the chef tapped on the door within minutes with their dinner. He pushed the silver cart over to the table for them.

Alley checked out the delicious smelling food. She didn't know why but she was starving. She saw the double chocolate cake sitting there and debated on whether she wanted to start with dessert first, but decided against it She took the lid off of her plate to see what they were having. Sitting on a plate was grilled tilapia with a lemon wedge on it. Steamed vegetables and garlic bread sat beside the fish. She sat down and ate her entire dinner.

"Are you sure you are feeling alright? You look a little pale.

"I'm sure I'll be fine. The doctor should be here any minute. I'll let you know what he says after he examines me."

Alley went into the bathroom to splash her face with water before the doctor arrived.

The knock on the door triggered her nerves. *What if something is wrong?*

"Your Majesty, I hear you aren't feeling well. What's going on?"

Alley waved him to the sitting area. "Come in doctor. I'm not feeling well. My stomach feels queasy and my head hurts."

The doctor opened his bag and checked her over thoroughly then smiled and said. "You're pregnant, Queen Alley."

"What?" Alley was in shock.

"Yes Your Highness, you are having a baby."

Alley thanked the doctor and saw him out. She gazed in the mirror, amazed. Her hand went to her stomach instantly. She was going to be a mother.

Evan opened the door and saw her standing there. "Is everything okay? What did the doctor say?" He was scared to death that he was going to lose her.

"I'm fine. The reason that I've been feeling so bad is that I'm carrying the heir to the throne."

"What?" Evan stood there

motionless for a minute, then. Then his eyebrows shot up.   Alley jumped up and down. "I'm pregnant. No more wine for me with our late night baths." She laughed.

"I'm going to be a father?" Evan couldn't believe it. He was completely amazed but scared too. "Alley you can't risk your life and our child's life battling Esmeralda. The plan must change."

"We have to stop her or our child will always be at risk."

"I know Alley, but I need to be the one to fight the battle. It's too risky. I'll cross through the portal, get her to follow me and I will be the one to destroy her. I don't want you anywhere around her when the time comes.

Alley was worried for Evan, but she agreed. They had a child to think about now and that child had to come first above all else.

It was getting late so Alley decided to get changed for bed. She got out her long white nightgown and slipped it over her head. Evan followed right behind her. She snuggled up on his chest and fell fast asleep.

The next day Alley and Evan set their plan into action.

"Alley you need to have a good breakfast before we head out. The chef has everything set up in the dining room."

Alley walked into the dining room and the smell of scrambled eggs and bacon made her stomach growl. She hadn't realized she was as hungry as she was. She sat down to eat and the servant poured her a tall glass of freshly squeezed orange juice.

When they were finished eating Alley and Evan left to set their trap in motion. They climbed up on the horse drawn carriage and began their trip.

They traveled to the edge of Majestic Falls where some of Esmeralda's men always hung out. They brought the horses to a stop.

"Evan, are you sure you can get all the powers?"

"Yes, Alley, all I have to do is jump through the portal at the edge of the waterfall right at nightfall. When I get on the other side I'll grab the bag of magic that the warlock has waiting for me and then jump back through the portal. No problem. It will only take me a few minutes."

"That sounds great. You will then be the most powerful warlock in the land as well as the King. This will be perfect. Let's get back to the castle and finish our plans."

Evan got the horses going and as he looked back it was as he suspected. Two men had jumped on horses and raced off. He knew they were going straight to Esmeralda. The plan was working perfectly.

Chapter Six

The sun was setting. It was time for Evan to go to the portal.

"Father, you make sure nothing happens to him," Alley said as she dropped her hand to her stomach. Her nerves were shot.

"I will, dear. Don't you worry. We will be back before you know it."

Evan grabbed the bag full of potions and pulled the strap over his head. He approached Alley and gently kissed her lips as he laid his hand on her stomach.

As planned, Mathew stepped through the portal first so Esmeralda wouldn't see him.

Evan waited until he heard the evil queen walking up behind him, and then jumped through the portal.

Esmeralda followed Evan through the portal coming through the mirror on the other side at the farmhouse.

Evan yelled, "Now!" He threw the glass bottle containing the vanishing potion at Esmeralda. "You are finished.

You messed with the wrong King."

As Esmeralda melted in front of their eyes, she grabbed the mirror and pulled it to the ground. Glass shattered as she screamed, "If I can't go back then you can't go back." Within seconds she melted away to nothing.

Evan and Matthew didn't expect that turn of events.

"What do we do Mathew? She destroyed the portal."

Mathew scratched his head for a minute. "There must be another portal."

"We have to get a message to Alley." Evan was more concerned with Alley at the moment than his own predicament.

"We'll get out of this mess. Don't worry. "

Evan paced back and forth across the floor. He had to get back to Alley and his unborn child.

"Alley didn't get a chance to tell you. She's pregnant. You're going to be a grandpa."

Mathew stood there in shock. A grin came across his face. "A Grandpa? We will get back. Some way or another we will get back."

***

Alley could feel in her heart that something was wrong. Evan should have made it back by now. Something must have gone terribly wrong. She approached the round crystal on the table. Rubbing it with both hands, Alley watched as the image solidified. She could see her father and Evan in the bedroom of the farm house.

Evan, what happened?

Alley. I'm sorry. We're trapped. Esmeralda destroyed the portal. We threw the potion on her and as she died she smashed the mirror. I'm not sure how we can get home, but I promise you, I won't stop until I make it back to you and our child.

Alley felt her knees tremble. She heard Evan's voice as she did before. Their souls had always been able to talk to each other. They were meant to be together. She'd just made it back to Evan and now he was trapped in the mortal world. She had to do something to fix this.

Alley ran down the stairs to the

study where she found Catherine reading a book. "Mother! Something went wrong."

"What is it Alley?" Catherine jumped up and ran to her daughter.

"Esmeralda destroyed the portal right after they hit her with the potion. We have to find a way to get them back to us. Please have somebody find out who the most powerful warlock of Majestic Falls is and send for him immediately. We must figure out what we can do about this."

Catherine ran off to find help.

Hours later the butler came to Alley's room. "Queen Alley, Master Parker is here to see you."

"Thank you. Please see him to the study. I'll be right there."

Alley sat down the book of spells that she had been staring at for over an hour and hadn't read a single word. She stood, dusted her dress off and made her way to the study. As she walked into the study she saw a man standing by the book shelf. He was unique looking with straight black hair, with matching mustache and goatee.

Alley approached holding out her

hand. "Thank you for meeting with me today, Parker."

He accepted her hand and kissed it. "I'm at your service." He said with a smile.

"Please have a seat," Alley said as she pointed to the brown suede couch on the other side of the room. "I need to discuss something with you that I trust you would keep in confidence."

Parker joined her on the couch. "Yes, of course."

"Thank you. I need your help with something as I've been told that you are the most powerful warlock in all of our land."

Parker sat up a little straighter liking the fact his reputation had made it all the way to the queen. "What can I help you with, Your Majesty?"

"King Evan is trapped in the mortal world. He fought Esmeralda and won. She is no longer a threat to our people. However, she destroyed the portal in the process and now King Evan is trapped. I need to create a new portal for him and my father to use to get back to Majestic Falls. Can this be done?"

Parker was on the edge of his seat, an intrigued expression on his face. He stood and paced back and forth for several minutes rubbing his goatee. He turned to Alley. "Queen Alley. This can be done, but it will take some time."

"What do you mean?" Alley stood and walked over to Parker. Parker exhaled a sigh before beginning. "Queen Alley, this can be done, and yes I can do it, but it can only be done one time of the year...December 21st at Winter Solstice. It's the only time I can summon a new portal."

Alley's breath left her body in a whoosh. Her eyes welled with tears. She chewed her fingernails, as she thought. "December? Are you kidding? I am your Queen" She picked up a notebook and threw it across the floor.

Parker stepped back and bowed his head.

Alley looked over at Parker, shame causing the color to rise in her cheeks. "I'm sorry. I don't know what got into me. That won't happen again."

"Yes, Queen. I'm sorry to say, but if it gives you any comfort it will be done...in time."

Alley's hand dropped to her stomach. The thought of Evan missing the birth of their child saddened her deeply. She wiped a tear away from her eye and squared her shoulders. It wasn't the time for tears. She must make arrangements for the creation of the portal. "Thank you Parker. If we must wait until Winter Solstice then so be it. Please begin preparing for it."

Alley stood there alone in her room trying to wrap her mind around everything that had happened over the last several weeks. She'd found her way back to Evan and was carrying his child, but he wouldn't come back in time for his or her birth. Tears poured down her face. She let them come. She'd tried desperately as Queen to control her emotions, but this news was more than she could bear.

After a few moments, she sucked in a ragged breath and drew in the boundless emotions overtaking her. She had work to do. She uncovered her crystal ball and ran her hands back and forth above it for a few seconds, thoughts of

Evan entering her mind. Evan could send his thoughts without any devices, but Alley never was as strong as Evan. She needed to channel him through the ball.

Moments later Evan and her father appeared in the ball. She watched them pace back and forth for a few minutes. Through the crystal's power, she reached out to her husband with her mind.

Evan, we can reopen the portal but it can't be done until Winter Solstice. It will be months before you come back to me.

She watched Evan fall to his knees.

Mathew ran over to Evan. "What is it? What's wrong?"

Evan stood up and kicked at the pieces of shattered glass from his battle. "We can't go home until Winter Solstice. That's months away. We won't be there for the birth of your first grandchild."

"Oh Evan. I'm so sorry." Mathew said as he laid a hand on Evan's shoulder. "We'll get back to them though. We will."

Chapter Seven

Alley awoke early. She sat up and stretched her arms above her head. Her body ached with lack of sleep.

She pulled the covers back and started to get out of bed when a wave of nausea struck. "Oh no." She covered her mouth with a hand and ran to the bathroom. Morning sickness. She thought she wasn't far enough along for that, but apparently she was wrong.

When the heaving finally stopped, she rinsed her mouth out with mouthwash, brushed her teeth and then ran a bath. She thought maybe a hot bath would help calm her jittery stomach.

She filled the bath to the top with steamy hot water. Letting out a deep breath she sank into the water. She leaned her head against the fluffy pink bath pillow that lay against the back of the tub. The hot water flowed back and forth across her as she enjoyed the peace and quiet. She gathered her thoughts. The first order of business was to meet the townspeople who'd been affected by Esmeralda's rage. She must create a plan of action to help rebuild their homes. Hopefully, this project would help take her mind off of Evan's absence.

Begrudgingly, Alley stood up and reached for the towel hanging on the rack behind her. She wrapped it around her body and then stepped out of the tub. As she combed through her hair, her mind drifted back to Evan. She missed him more than anything.

Her hand went to her stomach. "It's okay, baby. Your daddy will be home soon."

She finished getting dressed and went to meet her mother to begin her work. The townspeople had to be reassured that everything was going to be alright.

Alley ordered her top advisors to gather as many townspeople as they could and gave letters to messengers to deliver to those who were far away.

That afternoon she appeared before her subjects. She hugged every child she could, and laid comforting hands on their parents, trying to ease their pain

Once she'd roamed through the crowd, Alley climbed to the platform that had been erected on the town square. She raised her hands and the crowd quieted out of respect for their beloved queen.

"I know everyone is scared and you have lost much because of Esmeralda's wrath. But she is gone now. Your King, my beloved husband, destroyed her!"

Cheers erupted through the crowd. Alley raised her hands and again the crowd settled down. "Let me assure you that plans are already in place to begin rebuilding. I promise you I'll do all I can to erase from our memories the damage Esmeralda has caused."

More cheers warmed Alley's heart. Her people were good and kind and did not deserve all they had suffered. She would take care of them.

"Every able-bodied man who wants to help with this project line up over here and you will be paid for your services. I will pay your wages out of my own personal coffers. We will rebuild every house destroyed. If those of you with undamaged houses could be so kind as to take in some guests that would be of great help to us. The palace will house the rest. I promise to get your houses rebuilt as soon as we can and we will start today."

The cheering of the town's people was deafening. Excitement filled the air.

* **

Over the next several months, Alley remained true to her word. The town's people re-built their lives and things returned to normal. The people were happy and that pleased Alley, but her own loss of Evan weighed on her daily as she grew with child. Rising from her bed on a cold November morning she walked to the bathroom and gazed into the mirror. She rested her hand on her growing stomach.

"Not much longer, little one," she said. She swiped at the tear that slid down her cheek. "You will arrive into this crazy world and then shortly thereafter we can bring your daddy home."

After readying herself for the day, Alley joined her mother in the nursery. They'd worked hard to prepare the room for the baby's arrival.

As they painted the walls a pale

yellow, Alley turned to her mother. "Thanks for all your help with the baby stuff. I know how hard it is for you to be without Dad. I miss Evan more than words can say."

"Oh, Alley." Catherine put her arms around her daughter. "It will be okay. We only have a few more days to go, honey."

"Oh!" Alley grabbed her stomach.

"Are you okay?"

"Oh. That hurts. I think it's time, Mother. You better get the doctor. I think your new grandbaby is ready to make an appearance."

Catherine ran to get the doctor. Alley smiled and rubbed her belly. She pulled a cord and one of the house servants helped her to her room.

For hours Alley labored to bring her child into the world with her mother by her side. With every push she cried out for her husband and longed for him to be with her. At last she heard the cry of her child as her baby was born.

The doctor handed Alley her beautiful baby boy.

Alley pulled him in close to her. "It's okay Evan Mathew. Your daddy will be home soon."

Alley saw Catherine wipe the tears away from her eyes. She knew her mother missed Mathew as much as she missed Evan.

Chapter Eight

At last the Winter Solstice was upon them and Alley prepared herself for Evan's return. She dressed baby Evan in the cutest outfit she had and covered him in a warm blanket. As she sent for the horse and carriage she called for Catherine.

When her mother arrived, Alley said, "Are you ready to go get your husband now?"

Catherine smiled. "Oh yes. Let's go."

"I have sent for Parker. He will meet us there to open the portal."

The driver helped them into the carriage and drove them to the meadow.

As the horses came to a stop she saw Parker standing in the meadow and a blue glowing light forming in front of him. She stepped down from the carriage and turned to get baby Evan as Catherine handed him down to her.

Alley held her baby close to her chest as she walked over to the portal to wait for Evan.

The glow of the light disappeared

in front of her.

"What's going on Parker? Where did it go?"

"Queen Alley, please don't worry. These things take a few minutes. There is nothing wrong."

Alley's heart was rapidly beating. She felt as if it was going to jump out of her chest at any moment. She watched as another glowing light formed. This time it was bigger and it continued to get brighter every second it burned.

Within minutes Evan and Mathew walked through the portal.

Evan saw Alley standing there holding their child and tears flooded his face. He dashed through the portal to reach his wife and son. He swept them both into a warm hug. "Alley, he's beautiful. I love you more than words can say."

"I love you too, Evan." She glanced down at their son. "Meet Evan Mathew, your son."

Evan kissed Alley gently on the lips. "I will never leave you again."

The End

100% of all of the proceeds of this book will be given to:

The Epilepsy Foundation

Their National Office's location is:

Mailing Address:
Epilepsy Foundation
8301 Professional Place East,
Suite 200
Landover, MD 20785-2353
Telephone: 1-800-332-1000